D0835750

Ghostly Tales

by Susan Price
illustrated by Peter Stevenson

Contents

British Library Cataloguing in Publication Data

Price, Susan
    Ghostly tales.—(Mystery and adventure).
    I. Title   II. Stevenson, Peter, *1953-*
    III. Series
    823'.914[J]   PZ7
    ISBN 0-7214-0999-7

First edition

Published by Ladybird Books Ltd Loughborough Leicestershire UK
Ladybird Books Inc Lewiston Maine 04240 USA

© LADYBIRD BOOKS LTD MCMLXXXVII

Printed in England

Russell's bogle

RUSSELL'S BOGLE

Bogles live under floorboards, and up chimneys, and in outhouses and the back of cupboards. They're a sort of ghost, or maybe a sort of goblin. Or a mixture of the two. They're more solid than a ghost because they can pick things up and move them, but they're certainly not human. If you get a good one living in your house, life can be easy, because, if you leave them a bowl of milk and some bread every night, they'll do work for you. They'll sweep the floors, do the washing up, clean the windows – or, if you live on a farm, they'll cut hay and corn, groom horses, and collect eggs.

Some of them are a bit contrary. If you leave the house in a mess when you go to bed, and provided there's a bowl of milk and some bread in the middle of the mess, they'll eat the bread, drink the milk, and tidy the house up. But if you leave the house tidy, they'll drink the milk, eat the bread, and put everything where it shouldn't be – ashes on the floor, rubbish in the chairs, coals in the bread-oven and the cat in the dairy.

Some bogles are just bad, and a nuisance. They blow out the fire, smash crockery, sour milk, turn eggs bad, pull the bedclothes off sleeping people, hammer on the roof to wake everyone up – and every other bad turn and trick there is.

There was a farmer once, named Jim Russell, who was plagued by one of these malicious bogles. He wasn't married, and he had a hard job, managing the little farm his parents had left him on his own. The bogle came with the farm. It had been there longer than the Russells had, and was once a good, helpful bogle. Then one of Jim's ancestors had thanked it for harvesting his crops in a single night, and the bogle had held this against the whole family ever since. Bogles hate being thanked for anything. No one knows why. They just do; it's their way. Sometimes, if you thank a bogle, they sulk, go away and never

come back. But this bogle had stayed for revenge. It had tormented every Russell who had worked that farm for a hundred years, all because one Russell had been unable to keep his mouth shut on 'thank you'.

While Jim's father had been alive, Jim hadn't suffered too much, because the bogle had pestered his father. Once *he* became the farmer, however, Jim never got a good night's sleep. If the bogle wasn't pulling at his bedclothes, or scratching his headboard, or hammering on the wall above his head, then Jim was too worried about what it *was* doing to get any sleep.

If the bogle left him alone he knew that, when he got up in the morning, he was going to find his horses' manes and tails tied in tangles and knots, and their hides all lathered with sweat from the bogle's riding; or he was going to find the cows milked and the milk spoilt; or his whole house overturned, with no piece of furniture standing on its legs and every cupboard and drawer emptied of its contents.

Jim couldn't stop the bogle doing anything it wanted to do. It was stronger than he was. If he stayed in the house, it went to the stables; if he stood guard in the stables, it went to the cow-shed; if he went there, then the bogle took itself off to his barn, or back to the house.

People told him to hang stones with holes in them over the horses' stalls, to keep the bogle away; or rowan branches, or red thread – but none of that worked, because the bogle had been at the farm before the Russell family. It had a right to be there. The place was even called Bogle's Hole Farm. The bogle just tore down the stones and the branches and the thread; then it took the horses' shoes off and put them on again back to front.

No one could make a farm pay with this kind of thing going on. Jim couldn't make money from milk because the bogle so often spoiled it; he had no crops to sell, because the bogle carried his harvest over the countryside, dumping it in rivers and other people's yards. No one wanted to buy his animals, because they were so nervous and skinny after being harried by the bogle. Jim knew that he was soon going to be penniless; the bogle seemed to hate him more than any other Russell, even more than the one who had thanked it.

So Jim moved away from the farm, and went to stay with relatives in town. The bogle

followed him, but it didn't make such a nuisance of itself – after all, Jim's relatives were Robertsons not Russells, and the bogle had nothing against them.

For nights at a time it left Jim and the Robertsons alone, while it went back to the farm and looked after things there. The bogle kept the land and animals well, as if it had only wanted the farm to itself all along. Jim crept back there from time to time, at midday, to see how things were, and he found that the animals were all putting on weight, and seemed calm and contented; while everything else was in perfect repair and order.

It was maddening to see the bogle managing things the way Jim would have done himself, if he'd ever been given the chance. He loved the old farm and would have liked to have stayed, but he knew the bogle would never let him live in peace there. So he secretly sold all the animals at the best prices he could get. He thought the bogle would make trouble when he went to the farm with the drovers to take the animals away, but they saw and heard nothing of it.

The next thing Jim did was to sell the farm and house, furniture, machinery and all. He had to take a low price, but he didn't care. He wanted to get as far away from the Bogle's Hole as he could, and start again in some place where he could be the good farmer he knew he really was, instead of the poor, bogle-haunted fool that everyone pointed out, laughed at, and told stories about. So he borrowed money from his relatives, to add to that he had raised by the sales, bought himself a passage on a ship, and sailed away to Canada, leaving everything behind, and good riddance to it.

Once in Montreal, he went to a land-agent, to buy a new farm; but he had so little money that the only land he could buy was unclaimed land, not the best, out in the wilds, where he would have to work himself to a shadow to prepare the ground before he could even begin farming.

But if that was all he could afford, that was what he would have to have. And he was capable of catching himself fish and rabbits and such, and going a little hungry while he made a start. So he bought the land, and gave the deeds to a bank in return for money to buy supplies and tools, and a pack pony. When he had everything he needed, he loaded the pony and set off into the wilds.

It was a long, hard journey. He had to go through forests where no one had ever been

before, and that was constant, hard, hot work. He had to cross rivers without bridges, getting soaked, and then frozen by the wind. He had to climb mountains, and find his way by a map, because there were no signposts, and no one to tell him the way.

He was afraid of bears and wolves, and worried all the time that he was lost – and yet he was happy, because he was rid of the bogle, and he knew life would be better from now on. And, after three weeks of hard travelling, his map told him that he had found his way to the acres that were his.

He looked down on it from a hill, and he could see straightaway where the best place to build a house would be – near the stream, but slightly above it, so that it wouldn't be too damp. That's where he would set up his tent for now. He led his pack pony down to the spot.

He got his tent set up before nightfall, and set water to boil over his fire, to make porridge and tea. He lay on his back with his hands behind his neck, and sighed. It was nice to be home at last.

A voice spoke in the dusk. 'It took you long enough to get here,' said the bogle. 'I'll teach you to keep me waiting.' And it blew out his fire.

Never thank a bogle. You might not be the only one to suffer for it.

Granny Bunn

GRANNY BUNN

In the old days people used to go hunting hares. They used to set the dogs to chase them, while the men ran after on foot. Joel Wheeler was a miner, who loved hunting hares. He used to take his dogs out after hares every chance he got, and there were always plenty of other men who wanted to run their dogs, too. They soon made hares rare in their

neighbourhood. The men would take the dogs out and walk over the hills all day, and never see a hare.

Then Granny Bunn's grandson, Tommy, met them. 'You want a hare to hunt?' he asked. 'I can find you a hare.'

Most of the men were pleased, and said they'd give him a shilling if he could. 'I want three shillings,' said Tommy. 'You can easy raise it between you all.'

Now the men weren't quite so pleased, but Joel Wheeler gave the boy three shillings out of his pocket to find a hare.

'I saw one this morning,' said the boy. 'Come on!' And he ran off. Now all those men were good runners. You get lots of practice in running if you chase hares. But Tommy Bunn could outrun all of them. Not even all the dogs could keep up with him. 'He runs like a hare himself!' Joel Wheeler shouted.

Before they'd run half a mile, a hare jumped up in front of them. 'There's your hare!' shouted Tommy, but the dogs had seen it before he spoke, and they were away, the whippets and the lurchers, coursing through the heather and bilberries, with the men panting behind. They had a good chase that day, the first for weeks, even though the hare did get away.

Whenever they had trouble finding a hare after that, they asked Tommy Bunn to find one for them, and he always did, if they paid him first, and they always had a good, long chase. But they never caught a hare that Tommy Bunn found.

Some of the men started to take their dogs home if they came to the hunt and Tommy Bunn was there. When their friends asked why, they said, 'They're strange people, those Bunns. We want nothing to do with them.'

'Don't talk such rubbish!' Joel said. But half the hunt would go home, saying what was the good of a chase if you never caught the hare?

Joel thought the hares got away because the dogs in his hunt weren't good enough. So he walked over to the next village to see his friend, Dick Hanley.

Dick owned a famous dog named Flyer, because she was so fast. She was the best dog in six counties. Dick brought Flyer to the next hunt.

When Tommy Bunn saw Flyer, he said that he hadn't been able to find a hare, and they might as well all go home. Joel wouldn't have that. 'You've found us a hare every other time,' he said, and he caught hold of Tommy by the collar and insisted that he earn his three shillings.

So Tommy led them off over the hills and, just as always, a hare jumped up in front of them and began running for its life – and Tommy ran as if he was being hunted, too. He ran so fast that he was side by side with the hare. And right behind them was Flyer.

The hare looked behind her and saw the dog's open mouth, and zigged, and zagged to escape, but Flyer zigged and zagged too, and snapped her teeth a half-inch from the hare's foot. Some of the men, those who had the breath, cheered, because they saw that *this* hare wasn't going to escape from *this* dog.

Tommy Bunn was still up with the hare and the dog, but the animals had run away to the left of him, higher up the slope.

Tommy started shouting and waving his arms, as if he were calling to someone near the hare. The panting men running behind couldn't see who he was calling to – but the hare zagged again and began running down the hill towards Tommy – and Tommy shouted all the more. Flyer was on the hare's tail, and turned with the hare as neatly as if she were tied to it, and she snapped her teeth closed on the hare's hind foot.

The hare screamed and screamed – a terrible sound – and Tommy Bunn, ran up the hill towards the hare and the dog, shouting at the top of his voice. The dog was so surprised that it threw up its head to look at the boy, and let the hare go – and the hare darted forward and leapt into the boy's arms. Tommy wrapped the hare in his jacket and ran away downhill.

The men stopped running and stood gasping for breath, watching the boy go. From the hillside they watched him go all the way to the house where he lived with his Granny. The dogs came round them, even Flyer, wagging their tails and hoping their masters would tell them what to do, because they didn't know.

'What – do you make – of that?' Joel asked, when he had the breath. But no matter what the others thought of it, none of them could say anything, they were panting so hard.

After a while Joel started off down the hill, and all the others, dogs and men, followed him, though some of them were so tired they had to lean together. Joel led them to the poor little house where Tommy Bunn lived with his Granny. Joel knocked, and went into the kitchen. Not everyone followed him in. A lot of the men were afraid of Granny Bunn. The dogs stayed in the yard, whining.

Granny Bunn was sitting by the fire, and Tommy was kneeling in front of her, winding a bandage round her foot. Beside him was a bowl of reddened water, as if he'd just washed a wound.

'Come in, gentlemen, come in! Did you have a good hunt?' the old woman asked.

They took off their caps, and Joel said, 'We did, thanks. Have you hurt your foot?'

'I'm a clumsy old fool,' said Granny Bunn. 'I dropped a knife on it. Thank goodness I've got Tommy; he looks after his old Granny. Will you have a cup of tea with us? Tommy, put the kettle on.'

'Don't bother!' Joel said. 'Don't bother for us. We're just going.' And Joel backed out of the kitchen, and all the others went with him. Joel had meant to ask for his three shillings back, since Tommy had taken the hare, but in front of Granny Bunn, he didn't dare.

As they hurried away from the little house,

one of the men, who'd been running close
behind Tommy, but had been too out of
breath to speak before, said, 'Did you hear
what Tommy was shouting?'

'Shouting? When?' Joel asked.

'When the dog was close on the hare and
Tommy started shouting and waving. "Run,
Gran, run!" That's what he shouted.'

They all stopped in the road, with the dogs pressing against their legs, and looked at each other.

'Run, Gran, run!' he shouted – and the hare ran to him and jumped into his arms.

Joel was still a moment, then he took off at a run, and when he started running, so did everybody else, all those men, and all those dogs, running as if *they* were hares with dogs after them, running as far away from Granny Bunn and her grandson as they could get, as fast as they could go.

The doctor's dog

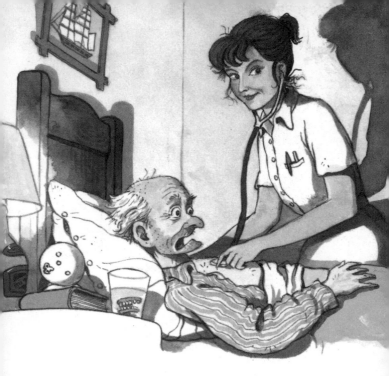

THE DOCTOR'S DOG

Doctor Glazebrook used to be our doctor.
She was a bit special because she was the
doctor that the police called out if they had
someone who needed medical treatment. They
used to call her up at all hours, but she was
used to that. People would telephone her and
ask her to come and look at a spotty baby, or
a relative who'd come over all peculiar, or
fallen off a chair, or turned a funny colour. So
Doctor Glazebrook would put her bag and
Thane in the car and off she'd go.

Thane was her dog. He wasn't an ordinary dog. He frightened the life out of most people the first time they saw him – which didn't do them much good if they were ill, but Doctor Glazebrook would rather her patients had died of shock than leave Thane behind. Thane was a deerhound.

That meant that he could put his front paws on the shoulders of a tall man as easily as other dogs would put them on a man's knee – and Thane would still be a head taller than the man. He was enormous, and heavy, and grey and shaggy, with long, long white teeth. A lot of people thought he was a wolf, but wolves are never so big.

Thane ate four pounds of meat a day and needed hours of exercise, which is why the doctor took him everywhere with her. She got

up early to take him a walk every morning, and on Saturdays and Sundays she took him for long walks in the country, hoping that no one would call her out for an emergency.

Doctor Glazebrook had bought Thane because she lived alone, and because she often had to go alone, at night, to places where you never quite knew who might be around. She thought she'd feel safer if she had a big dog, so she went full measure and bought one of the biggest dogs ever heard of.

Thane was really very gentle and affectionate, and was always trying to climb onto Doctor Glazebrook's lap for a cuddle, but he didn't look like that kind of dog at all. And he never barked, or made much noise moving about. If you knocked at Doctor Glazebrook's door, she would open it and then, suddenly, there would be this huge shaggy thing breathing in your face and showing its teeth. You didn't get any warning at all. People used to jump out of their shoes.

Thane would lie on the floor of the doctor's surgery while she was seeing patients, and if *she* moved towards a patient to examine them, that was okay. Thane would just watch with one eye, and perhaps thump his tail on the floor. But if a *patient* moved towards the doctor, no matter what the reason, Thane would lift up his front end very suddenly, and show his teeth. He wouldn't growl – but the patient would sit well back in his chair and freeze. Thane just wasn't a dog you felt like taking risks with. There was too much of him.

Then Thane died. He was old, and despite all the care Doctor Glazebrook took of him, his heart gave out.

Doctor Glazebrook was so upset she had to take time off work. She had really loved that dog, and it was years, really, before she got over his dying. She'd owned dogs before, she said, but never one like Thane, never one so special, and intelligent, and loving.

While Thane had been around, she said, she'd never felt lonely or nervous, either at

home, or travelling about late at night. 'If I'd
had a special guard of your men following me
about I couldn't have felt safer,' she told the
Police Inspector.

'You'll be getting a new dog, then?' the
Inspector asked.

'Oh no,' Doctor Glazebrook said. 'I don't
think so. Well, not for a while anyway. Not
after Thane. He was too special.'

Even two years later, Doctor Glazebrook hadn't got another dog. If you went to see her at her surgery, you'd go in expecting there to be a big grey shape lying on the floor near her desk, taking up most of the room, and when there wasn't, you felt uneasy, somehow, about that empty space. You'd keep looking at it. The trees outside the window would throw moving shadows on the floor and you'd look, quick, thinking you'd seen Thane move – but there'd just be the yellow carpet, bare and vacuumed clean of dog-hairs. Doctor Glazebrook got a bit fed up of people asking her when she was going to get another dog. 'I don't feel I need one any more,' she said. 'You know, when Thane died, I thought I'd be nervous without him, but I'm not, not a bit.'

'Maybe he's still with you,' I said to her, once.

'Now don't go starting silly rumours like that,' she said.

Then came the night the police sent a car for her, because a man they'd arrested needed medical treatment. She thought the man looked at her oddly when she went into the room where they were holding him; the kind of look someone gives you when they think they know you, but aren't sure. But Doctor Glazebrook didn't know this man, so she took no notice. While she was stitching him up, he said. 'You went to that cash dispenser the

other night, didn't you? The one outside the bank in the High Street.'

'What of it?' Doctor Glazebrook asked.

'I saw you,' he said. 'I saw all that money you got out...Fancy you being the one to patch me up. If you hadn't had that big dog with you, I'd have had that money.'

'What dog?' Doctor Glazebrook shouted. The man was startled.

'Your dog! The dog with you! Biggest dog I ever saw. It was like a ruddy wolf.'

'I didn't have a dog with me,' Doctor Glazebrook said.

'Yes, you did!' the man said, getting a bit angry. 'A big, grey dog. It followed you up to the dispenser, and sat by you while you got the money, and then it followed you off to your car...And it gave me a kind of look, so I knew I wasn't going to try anything. A dog that size could eat you.'

Doctor Glazebrook finished treating the man, and then felt she needed treatment herself. The police gave her a cup of hot tea and a comfortable chair in an office, to sit down for a while. 'You come over a bit faint, Doctor?' a young constable asked her. She said yes. She wasn't going to tell the police the real reason, because she reckoned they'd think she was mad – which was daft because the police are always being called out to investigate ghosts and poltergeists.

The doctor went home and sat alone in her
house, in the dark, and she wondered about
how she always felt quite happy like that, as if
she had company. She said, aloud, 'Thane!'
and, amongst all the other creaks and noises
of the house, she heard a thump-thump, as if a
big, heavy dog's tail was beating on the carpet.

She came to see me once, when I had 'flu. I asked her if she was ever going to get another dog, and she told me all this to explain why she wasn't. 'I don't need one, you see,' she said. 'And anyway, how could I get another dog? Thane might not like it, and he's so good, I'd hate to upset him.'

I looked very carefully at the empty air all round her, when she left to go back to her surgery, but I couldn't see anything – and you'd think Thane would be easy enough to spot, even as a ghost. But whenever I go to Doctor Glazebrook's surgery now, I can't look at anything except that empty patch of carpet by her desk. The way the shadows move over it – they make you see things from the corner of your eye.